Greedy Goat

With much love to CC

First published in hardback in Great Britain by HarperCollins Publishers Ltd in 1999
First published in Picture Lions in 2000

1 3 5 7 9 10 8 6 4 2
ISBN: 0 00 6646689

Picture Lions is an imprint of the Children's Division, part of HarperCollins Publishers Ltd.
Copyright © Colin and Jacqui Hawkins 1999
The authors assert the moral right to be identified as the authors of the work.

The HarperCollins website address is: www.fireandwater.com

Printed in Singapore by Imago

Greedy Goat

Colin and Jacqui Hawkins

PictureLions
An Imprint of HarperCollins*Publishers*

This is Greedy Goat.

Greedy Goat was always eating. Every day she ate a HUGE breakfast,

a HUGE lunch,
and a HUGE dinner.

She also ate lots of snacks in between!

When Greedy Goat got really hungry,
she would eat almost anything.
One day, she even ate
Daft Dog's glasses.
CRUNCH!

Another day, she
chewed big holes in
Mrs Cow's washing.
It put Mrs Cow in a
very bad M O O O D !

Every day, Greedy Goat went to the supermarket and did her shopping.

Greedy Goat bought
so much food that
her bills were
HUGE!

Before long Greedy Goat became very
poor. Her clothes were old and patchy,
and her house was very shabby, especially
as Greedy Goat nibbled her sleeves and
chewed at the sofa and curtains.

Greedy Goat went to the bank to borrow some money. But Mr Cow, the bank manager, said, "NOOO!" He thought that Greedy Goat would eat up all his money.

"Why don't you get a job, Greedy Goat?" asked Mr Cow. "What can you dooo?"

Greedy Goat thought very hard – the thing she did best was EAT! So she started the *Greedy Goat Lawn-Munching and Garden-Nibbling Service.*

Every day Greedy Goat set off for work in
her mobile garden shed. In each garden she
would munch the lawn very short, then nibble
the shrubs and bushes until they were neat
and tidy. Greedy Goat loved her work.

Greedy Goat's Garden Service
was such a HUGE success
that she soon needed
lots of helpers.
She got the sheep
to nibble the grass,

the birds to tidy up
the window boxes,

the Barker Boys
to do the
digging,

G. G. Horse
to prune
the trees and
Dotty Donkey
to trim the
hedges.

With so much to do,
Greedy Goat was
always on the go.

Before long, the *Greedy Goat Lawn-Munching and Garden-Nibbling Service* became HUGE!
Greedy Goat became HUGELY rich,
HUGELY famous,

HUGELY happy...

and, of course, being Greedy Goat,
she was still HUGELY HUNGRY!